DREAMWORKS
KUNG FU PANDA 3

Movie Novelization
adapted by Tracey West

Simon Spotlight

New York London Toronto Sydney New Delhi

SIMON SPOTLIGHT
An imprint of Simon & Schuster Children's Publishing Division
1230 Avenue of the Americas, New York, New York 10020
This Simon Spotlight paperback edition December 2015
Kung Fu Panda 3 © 2015 DreamWorks Animation LLC. All Rights Reserved.
All rights reserved, including the right of reproduction in whole or in part in any form.
SIMON SPOTLIGHT and colophon are registered trademarks of Simon & Schuster, Inc.
For information about special discounts for bulk purchases, please contact Simon & Schuster Special Sales at 1-866-506-1949 or business@simonandschuster.com.
Manufactured in the United States of America 1115 OFF
10 9 8 7 6 5 4 3 2 1
ISBN 978-1-4814-4116-2
ISBN 978-1-4814-4117-9 (eBook)

CHAPTER 1
Battle in the Spirit Realm

Master Oogway sat on top of a mountain floating among the white, fluffy clouds of the Spirit Realm, peacefully meditating with his eyes closed. Peach blossom petals fell from above and landed on his face, tickling his nose.

"Inner peace, inner peace, itchy nose," he chanted, sneezing the petal away. "Inner peace."

Two curved blades made of jade, each one attached to a chain, suddenly whizzed through the air toward him. Without opening his eyes, Oogway quickly grabbed the nearest one and sent it flying into the other blade, knocking them both down.

Oogway opened his eyes to see a massive, muscled yak coming through the clouds toward him, his whole body glowing green with energy. His head was crowned by two huge horns. His black mane hung down his back, and the chains of his blade weapons were wrapped around his wrists.

"Kai, old friend," Oogway calmly greeted him.

"Master Oogway," said Kai, his voice as dark and deep as the look in his eyes.

"Our battle ended five hundred years ago," said Oogway.

Kai's angry eyes blazed. "Well, now I'm ready for a rematch."

He launched himself through the air at Oogway, slicing through the mountain to reach the tortoise. Chunks of the mountain floated away.

"YAAAA!" he cried.

He sent the two blades hurtling through the air once more. This time Oogway leaped out of the way, swiftly dodging them.

"You've grown stronger," Oogway remarked.

He quickly moved his hands, and the shape of a glowing Chinese symbol appeared in the air in front of him. The symbol flew toward Kai, knocking him down. But Kai jumped right back up.

"After five hundred years in the Spirit Realm, you pick up a thing or two," Kai explained, with the hint of a grin on his face. He looked down at the belt around his waist. Several jade amulets dangled from it.

Oogway stared at the amulets, recognizing the animal shapes of his former students who had ascended into the Spirit Realm. What terrible thing had Kai done?

"I have taken the chi of every master here. And soon I will have your power too," he boasted.

"When will you realize," Oogway said calmly, "the more you take, the less you have?"

Kai launched his chain blades once again. They latched on to floating chunks of mountain. Then he hurled the heavy chunks at Oogway.

Oogway moved his hands again, creating a shield in the air shaped like a yin-and-yang symbol.

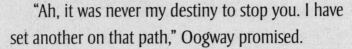

Smash! The chunks of mountain shattered the shield into pieces. The impact sent Oogway flying back as Kai's chains wrapped around him. Kai pulled Oogway closer to him.

Then Kai began to pull the green chi out of Oogway's body. As the energy left him, Oogway slowly turned to jade.

"With your chi I will finally be able to return to the mortal world," Kai said. "And this time you won't be there to stop me."

"Ah, it was never my destiny to stop you. I have set another on that path," Oogway promised.

Then the old master shriveled and shrank until all that was left of him was a small jade amulet. Kai hung it from a cord around his neck, instead of his belt. Everyone would see what he had done to the great Oogway.

Kai grinned at the amulet. "Then I will find him and take his chi too."

Kai let loose a wave of green chi, which enveloped him. A portal opened up between the Spirit Realm and the mortal realm, which took Kai all the way down to Earth.

CHAPTER 2
Po the Teacher?

The sun slowly rose over the Jade Palace, which sat high on a mountaintop overlooking the Valley of Peace. Every morning, when the villagers in the Valley woke up, they looked at the palace and knew they were safe.

For inside lived the best kung fu fighters in the land. Master Shifu, their leader. Tigress, Mantis, Monkey, Viper, and Crane: the Furious Five. And the Dragon Warrior himself, the mighty panda called Po.

That morning Po exploded through the doors of the bunkhouse.

"Justice! The most important meal of the day!" he cried as he bounded down the mountain toward the village.

The Furious Five followed him. Tigress moved with agile grace. Monkey propelled himself with his long arms. Mantis hopped with amazing speed. Viper's body smoothly glided down the rocks. And Crane soared above them all.

They landed awesomely . . . in front of Mr. Ping's noodle shop. "Let's have, um, two spring rolls—" Po began, placing their order.

"Three," Monkey cut in.

"Spicy tofu bun," added Crane.

"The spicy noodle soup for Tigress," Po put in. "Did you want extra sauce for that?"

"She wants it on the side," Monkey said.

"On the side," Tigress confirmed, crossing her arms.

Once they had their lunch, Po and the Furious Five ran through the valley once again as villagers called from windows and gathered on the streets.

"Go, Dragon Warrior!" they cheered. "Defend our valley!"

Po and the Five sprinted and jumped, darting between their adoring fans. Then Po led them back up the mountain.

"Yee-ha!" Po cheered, striking a dramatic kung fu pose as he landed back outside the Jade Palace. But, looking around, he saw the others weren't posing with him. "You guys aren't doing the dramatic pose, are you?"

"I'm doing the dramatic slouch," Crane said.

"You guys, never underestimate the power of the dramatic entrance," Po told them. "I've heard of some masters who could win a fight just by throwing open a door. Shuh-sha!"

He moved to kick open the door of the training hall when Master Shifu stepped in front of him.

"Dramatic entrance?" Master Shifu asked, raising an eyebrow. A red panda, Master Shifu barely came up to Po's waist—but he could topple the big panda with just one look.

"Master Shifu, I, uh . . . ," Po began, embarrassed.

"The Dragon Warrior is correct!" Master Shifu interrupted, surprising Po. "Before the battle of the fist comes the battle of the mind. Hence . . . the dramatic entrance."

Master Shifu turned and leaped through the doors to the training hall. Rows of crossbow-wielding geese fired flaming arrows, lighting the cauldrons that lined the hall.

Poof! They exploded into flames.

"Whoa, nice dramatic entrance," said Po, impressed. "What's the occasion?"

"Today will be my final class," Master Shifu replied.

"Your final . . . Wait, I didn't even know you were sick!" Po said. "Although you have been looking a little—"

"I'm not sick!" Master Shifu protested.

"—healthy. A little healthy. A *lot*, actually," Po said, trying to recover.

Master Shifu took a deep breath. "My final class, because from now on, your training will be in the hands of the Dragon Warrior!"

The Furious Five looked at Master Shifu like he was crazy.

"WHAT?!" Po shouted, once he realized what Master Shifu had said. He leaned over and whispered loudly into Master Shifu's ear, "Me? Teach? I mean, why not Tigress? She's always telling everyone what to do."

"Be quiet, Po," Tigress commanded.

"See what I mean?" Po asked.

"Tigress is not the Dragon Warrior. You are," Master Shifu replied firmly.

A feeling of panic started to well inside Po. Before he became the Dragon Warrior, he was just a humble noodle-shop server who looked up to the Furious Five as his heroes. Then Master Shifu had taught him how to harness his inner strength to perform feats of amazing awesomeness, and he had become a kung fu hero too. Fighting evil bad guys? That came easy to him now. But *teaching* . . .

"Come on, they're the Five," Po said. "What could I teach them?"

"There is always something more to learn, even for a master," Master Shifu replied. "For instance, let me show you another move . . . the dramatic exit."

Master Shifu pointed his staff across the hall. "What's that?!" he cried.

Po and the Furious Five turned to look, and when they turned back, Master Shifu was gone.

"Where'd he go?!" Po asked.

Then he noticed that the Furious Five were all standing at attention.

"Master," they said, bowing to Po.

"We await your instructions, Master," Crane said.

"All you have to lose is our respect," Tigress said, her golden eyes fixed on him.

Po gulped. How could he possibly teach the Furious Five?

But he had to try. Master Shifu had asked him to do it.

Mantis turned to Po hopefully. "Seriously, how bad can it be?"

A few minutes later Mantis had his answer: "Very bad! Very, very bad!"

The Training Hall was set up like an extreme obstacle course. Sharp blades, when set in motion, swung like pendulums. Arrows whizzed across the hall at unexpected moments. Flames shot up as if out of nowhere.

Po was nervously calling out commands from Master Shifu's seat as the Furious Five jumped and flew through the course.

"Monkey, Immovable Mountain Stance!" he yelled.

"Yes, Master," Monkey replied. He froze atop one of the Training Hall machines, motionless, until . . .

Crunch! Monkey fell into the gears of the machine.

"Uh, I mean . . ." Po turned to the other four. "Tigress, Tornado Backflip!"

"Yes, Master," Tigress said dutifully. She flipped backward—right into a giant swinging ball of fire.

"Oh, fire!" Po cried in alarm.

"Fire!" repeated the crossbow-wielding geese.

The geese shot their arrows at Tigress.

"Sorry!" Po yelled, as one hit her in the butt. "Crane, go high, I mean, low! Oh!"

Crane swooped high and then dipped low—just as Viper was speeding past. She clotheslined him and he landed on tiny Mantis.

"Ah! My claw thingy!" Mantis cried.

Po tried to make things better by shouting more commands.

"Totem Pole Poison Technique! Swarming Insect Bite with Yellow Tail, Yellow Jacket, spicy . . ."

"Oof!"

"Ow!"

"Ouch!"

The cries of the Furious Five rang through the palace as Po's directions kept causing them to crash into obstacles—and into one another.

Exhausted and beaten up, the Furious Five fell into a tangled heap on the training room floor.

"Good job, Po," Viper groaned, trying to be encouraging.

"Did you at least learn a *little* something?" Po asked, wincing.

"Yes," Tigress said. "I learned that you can't teach."

"And that Tigress is flammable," Crane added.

Po's face fell . . . then the roof of the Training Hall fell too.

CHAPTER 3
The Power of Chi

That evening Po walked sadly through the sculpture garden. He saw a few of the palace geese pass by and he hid.

"I'm glad we're not Po right now!" said one of the geese.

"What a loser!" said another.

"What was Shifu thinking?"

"What was Oogway thinking?"

Then they noticed Po hiding beside them.

"I think he heard us," one of the guards said.

"I didn't hear anything," Po replied, coming out of his hiding spot.

"He said you're a loser," the first guard said, toddling off with the others.

Po looked up at the statue of Oogway, the elderly tortoise who had been the senior master of the Jade Palace before Master Shifu. It was Oogway who had named Po the Dragon Warrior, shortly before he ascended into the Spirit Realm.

"Sorry, Oogway," Po said to the statue. He sighed, then turned to go and ran into Master Shifu.

"Ahh!" Po cried. "Would you stop doing that?"

"How was your first day teaching?" Master Shifu asked.

"Humiliating."

"I heard."

"Who told you? Did Tigress tell you?"

"I heard . . . the roof collapse, the cries of pain. And Tigress told me."

"Yeah, well, did she also tell you that it'll never happen again?" Po snapped. "Because I am done."

"Teaching? Or being humiliated?" Shifu asked.

"Both! I don't know why you ever thought I could teach that class."

Shifu looked at Po calmly. "If you only do what you can do, you will never be more than you are now."

"I don't wanna be more!" Po cried. "I like who I am."

Shifu shook his head. "*You* don't even know who *you* are."

"Of course I do," Po said. "I'm the Dragon Warrior."

"And what exactly does that mean, Dragon Warrior?"

"It means, you know, just going around and punching and kicking. Defending the Valley and stuff."

"Punching and kicking? You think that is what the great Master Oogway saw for you? A five-hundred-year-old prophesy fulfilled so you could spend your days 'kicking butt' and running through the town high-fiving bunnies?"

"Yes?" answered Po in a tiny voice.

"No!" Shifu said firmly. "Oogway saw greatness

in you, Po. Against my better judgment. More than you can see in yourself. Incredible power awaits you. Power beyond anything you can imagine."

Master Shifu stood up and began a series of slow, practiced movements. As he moved, a golden light began to gather in his hands. He brought his hands together and then directed the flowing energy toward a tiny flower bud at the base of the Oogway statue. The bud immediately opened to reveal a beautiful flower.

Po stared at him in wonder. "Whoa! What was that?"

"That was chi."

"Whoa . . . what's chi?" Po asked.

"The energy that flows through all living things," Master Shifu explained.

Po's eyes widened. "So . . . you're saying if I teach, I'll be able to do cool stuff like that?"

"No, I'm saying if you teach, then *I'll* be able to do cool stuff like that," Master Shifu replied. "Mastering chi requires mastery of self. Oogway sat alone in a cave for thirty years asking one question: 'Who am I?' I'm lucky if I get five minutes before you interrupt—"

"Aww, so now I have to sit alone in a cave for thirty years?" Po whined.

"Eventually. After you master teaching," Master Shifu said.

"Teaching?" Po asked. "There's no way I'm ever going to be like you."

"I'm not trying to turn you into me," Master Shifu said. "I'm trying to turn you into you."

He plucked the flower, handed it to Po, and walked off.

Po was more confused than before. "Turn me into me? Wait a second, that makes no—" He called after Master Shifu. "Almost there, Shifu! Just a little more confusing and you'll be the next Oogway!"

Po looked up at the Oogway statue. "Oh sorry, no offense, Master Oogway," he said. "I'll let you get back to your eternal peace."

CHAPTER 4
A Stranger in the Valley

Kaboom! A chi portal split open, carving a massive crater into the ground. Kai emerged from the glowing green portal, his eyes blazing with chi energy.

He had landed in a field being farmed by a rabbit and a goose. He shot out his blades to keep the farmers from fleeing. Terrified by the sight of Kai, the goose laid an egg.

"What is this place?" Kai asked.

"Uh . . . my brother's farm?" the rabbit ventured.

"Ah." Kai nodded. "If I stepped on you, would you die?"

The frightened goose dropped a few more eggs.

"Yes?" the rabbit replied nervously.

Kai grinned. "The mortal realm." He had returned, finally, after five hundred years!

He looked down at the Oogway amulet around his neck.

"You hear that, Oogway? I'm back," he said. He raised his muscled arms in the air. "Kai has returned!"

The rabbit and the goose looked blankly at each other.

"Who?" asked the rabbit.

"Kai. General Kai. Supreme Warlord of all China," Kai said.

The two farmers shrugged.

"The Jade Slayer. Master of Pain. You may know me as the Beast of Vengeance. Maker of Widows?" Kai tried.

The goose shook his head.

Kai sighed. "Okay. I used to work with Oogway."

The rabbit and goose lit up.

"Oh, Master Oogway! Now he was a great warrior!" said the rabbit.

The goose nodded. "Everyone knows Master Oogway. The wise and mighty—"

"Okay, enough," Kai said. He took several amulets from his belt and tossed them onto the ground. They transformed into kung fu masters made of jade.

"Find Oogway's students and bring them to me!" Kai ordered.

The jade masters, now under Kai's control, ran off. Kai lifted up Oogway's amulet.

"By the time I am done with them, Oogway, there will be no one left who will even remember your name. Kai is coming."

Ghostly green chi illuminated Kai's face as the rabbit and goose shivered with fear.

That same night, Po visited his dad's noodle shop. Mr. Ping was a goose who had adopted Po when he was just a baby. Through the years, he always made sure the growing panda had plenty of noodles and dumplings to eat. And he was always a good listener when Po was sad or worried.

Po was taking a bath with his kung fu action figures in a big wooden tub in the alley behind the noodle shop.

"Teach me? Oh no, it's the Dragon Teacher!" he made one action figure say.

"Class is in session! Wutaaiii!" he said with another.

Suddenly Mr. Ping burst in to the alley. Po jumped in surprise. "Oh hey, Dad! What's up? I was just stopping by for a little soak," he said, hiding the figurines underwater.

"Okay, what's wrong?" Mr. Ping asked.

"Nothing," Po lied. He casually shook some bath salts into the tub.

"Nothing? I come home to find you taking a bath with your dolls—"

"Action figures," Po corrected him.

"And instead of adding bath salts to the water,

you just added Szechuan peppercorns," Mr. Ping informed him.

Po yelped. "Szechuan—oh my tenders! Hot!" He quickly poured some cool water into the bath and sighed.

"Okay, yes, something's wrong," Po admitted.

"There, there, son. Tell your daddy all about it," said Mr. Ping gently as he grabbed a scrub brush and began scrubbing under Po's arm. "Lift your arm."

Po launched into his problem. "Shifu says I don't know what it means to be the Dragon Warrior. And now I have to be a teacher? I thought I finally knew who I was. If I'm not the Dragon Warrior . . . who am I?"

There was a heavy silence until his dad broke in. "A teacher? Teaching kung fu? Po, that's a promotion. Take the job, son! And someday, when you're in charge of the whole Jade Palace, I can sell noodles in the lobby. Woohoo!"

He turned back to Po. "Why are you still here taking a bath like a baby? Get out. Get up. Go, go, go! Franchise expansion awaits us!"

Mr. Ping hoisted Po out of the tub and began to towel him off.

"But what about the Dragon Warrior dumpling-eating contest? I have to defend my title!" Po reminded him.

"No one's going to beat your dumpling-eating record," Mr. Ping assured him.

A pig poked his head into the alley. "Someone's about to beat your dumpling-eating record!" he cried.

Po and Mr. Ping looked at each other in disbelief. They hurried into the restaurant. A crowd of villagers was gathered around someone and cheering, but Po couldn't see who was eating the dumplings.

"Go! Go! Go!" the pigs and rabbits chanted.

"Who's eating my dumplings?" Po demanded.

"And who's paying for them?" asked Mr. Ping.

They pushed through the crowd to see the back of a huge, vaguely familiar figure leaning over a table. He was picking up dumplings and stuffing them into his mouth faster than Po had ever thought possible.

"One hundred one, one hundred two!" the villagers counted.

The big stranger pounded his fist on the table. Then he leaped up and turned, his arms raised in triumph.

"One hundred and three! Yeah!" he cried, his mouth full of dumpling.

Po and Mr. Ping gasped. The stranger was a panda! A panda taller than Po and almost twice as wide!

Po was stunned. When he was just a baby, his village had been attacked. Po's mother had made sure he was safe, but Po believed he was the only survivor. No other panda had ever been seen in the valley for years.

"Who are you?" Po asked.

The stranger held up a finger, pounded his chest, and then swallowed his last bite of dumpling.

"I'm Li Shan. I'm looking for my son," he said.

Everyone gasped. The villagers all looked at Po. Mr. Ping looked at Po.

"You lost your son?" Po asked.

Li nodded. "Yes. Many years ago."

"I lost my father," Po said.

"I'm very sorry," said Li.

"Thank you," said Po.

"Well, good luck to you," said Li.

"You too," said Po. "I hope you find your son."

"And I hope you find your father."

Po and Li both turned to walk away. The bunnies and pigs shook their heads. The villagers looked back and forth from Po to Li. How could these two pandas not see the truth?

Then the two pandas stopped. Po looked at Li's green eyes. And his big belly. And furry feet. Li did the same thing.

"Son?" asked Li.

"Huh?" Po asked, still not quite getting it.

Li's eyes lit up. "Oh my gosh, it *is* you!"

Po gasped. He finally realized it! Li was his long-lost father!

"Well, don't just stand there! Give your old man a hug!" Li cried.

Po ran forward and threw himself into Li's arms. His father squeezed him in a big panda bear hug.

Mr. Ping watched them, his beak open in shock. The Po action figure he was holding fell from his hand and clattered to the floor.

"I can't believe you're alive!" Po said.

"I thought I'd lost you forever, Little Lotus," said Li, holding back tears.

Po backed out of the hug. "Oh, okay. This is very embarrassing, but I think you've got me confused with a panda named Lotus. My name is Po."

Li nodded. "Oh right, you wouldn't . . . Little Lotus was the name you were given at birth."

"Really?" asked Po. There was nothing little about Po at all. Or flowery, for that matter.

Li knew what his son was thinking. He laughed. "Really!"

Po shook his head. "I can't believe it. After all these years. And you're really here? This is amazing!"

Po turned to Mr. Ping. "Hey, Dad! Come say hi to . . ."

He stopped. Mr. Ping was his dad, but Li was his dad too, right? He turned to Li.

"Um," Po began, "I don't know what I'm supposed to call you."

"I'm pretty sure he said his name was Li," Mr. Ping said. There was a hint of suspicion in his voice.

Li pointed at Mr. Ping.

"You! Come here!" Li ordered in a booming voice.

Mr. Ping started to back away, but Li scooped him up in a hug. "Thank you. Thank you for taking such good care of my son."

Mr. Ping squirmed out of his grasp. "Your son? Now hold on just a minute." He looked at Po. "How do we know this stranger is even related to you?"

Po wasn't paying attention. He stood next to Li, and the two pandas were jiggling their massive bellies.

"Look at that. Our bellies could be brothers!" Li said proudly. "Hey, son, let me teach you how to Belly Gong."

He bumped bellies with Po, and both bellies began to bounce and wiggle.

"Belly Gong!" Li cried.

Po laughed. "That's so cool. They jiggle the same."

"It's like looking in a fat mirror," Li agreed.

Po pulled the village sketch artist from the crowd and asked him to draw the two of them. "I can't believe we're taking a picture together!" Po said excitedly. But when the artist handed them the sketch, Mr. Ping had sketch-bombed them.

"But I still don't understand," Mr. Ping interrupted. "I thought Po was the only panda left."

"No, there's a whole bunch of us," Li told him.

"Where?" Po asked, excitement rising in his voice.

Li bent down and whispered. "A secret Panda Village in the mountains."

"Whoa," said Po. "But how did you know where I was?"

"I received a message that led me here," Li replied.

The villagers began to gather around them. Everyone wanted to hear Li's story.

Mr. Ping's eyes narrowed. "How could you receive a message if no one could find you? Sounds suspicious to me."

The villagers nodded, and all eyes turned to Li.

"It was a message from the universe," Li said.

"Oooooooh," said the villagers.

"Whoa," said Po.

"Rats," muttered Mr. Ping.

"Now what's all this about a Dragon Warrior?" Li asked.

"How'd you know I was the Dragon Warrior?" Po asked. "Did the universe tell you that too?"

"No, the poster did," Li replied, pointing to the restaurant walls. Colorful posters selling DRAGON WARRIOR TOFU! and DRAGON WARRIOR SPICY NOODLES! decorated them.

"And the gift shop. I bought a cup!" Li said, holding up a tea mug with Po's face on it.

Po grinned. "There's so much to show you! You're going to be so awesomely proud! Come on! Come on!"

He grabbed Li's paw and dragged him outside the restaurant. Mr. Ping watched them go. A bunny picked up the Po action figure he had dropped and handed it back to him.

Mr. Ping stared at it. "I'm already awesomely proud," he mumbled sadly.

CHAPTER 5
The Hall of Heroes

Po led his father to the Jade Palace. They slowly climbed the countless steps going up the mountain.

"Couple . . . more . . . steps," Po said, panting.

"Give . . . me . . . a minute," Li panted along with him.

"Feeling the burn," Po admitted. "Do you have panda asthma too? Does that run in the family? Dad, you're going to love this. It's like the coolest thing ever."

When they finally reached the top of the mountain, Po swung open the massive doors of the Jade Palace. The only light in the room came from an altar lit with candles. They illuminated a smooth, jade floor. Tall jade columns carved with dragons lined both sides of the hall. And between the columns were wood pillars topped with beautiful, mysterious objects.

"This is the Hall of Heroes," he explained. "Home of the most priceless kung fu artifacts in all of China."

"Whoa!" Li exclaimed. "This place is—"

"Awesome? You were going to say 'awesome,' right? Because it totally is!" Po said.

"Totally!" Li agreed.

"But be super careful," Po warned. "Everything is very fragile here."

Po pointed to a beautiful urn with handles shaped like dragons. "Like the Urn of Whispering Warriors. Um, someone broke that once."

"Who?" asked Li.

Po looked up at the ceiling. "Some idiot."

He rushed to a suit of rhino armor.

Li was impressed. "Wow!"

"This is Master Flying Rhino's battle armor," Po explained.

"I wonder if I could fit in that," said Li.

"Get out of my head, Dad! I've wondered the same thing!"

"If I could fit in it?" Li asked.

"If *you* could? No. If *I* could fit," Po replied.

"Oh," said Li.

Po grabbed him by the hand again and dragged him from one treasure to another. He stopped in front of a row of tiny helmets.

"Dad, look at this! The battle helmets of Master Rat's army!" Po said.

Then he ran to dolphin-shaped armor mounted on the wall.

"This is my favorite. Master Dolphin's water-proof armor."

Po ran to a beautifully carved two-wheeled wagon with handles. "Check it out. It's the legend-ary battle rickshaw of Emperor Hawk!"

Li appeared behind Po, wearing Master Flying Rhino's armor.

"Sweet ride," he remarked. Po saw him and jumped back.

"Dad! What are you doing? We're not supposed to touch anything!" Po reminded him.

"Oh! Sorry, sorry," Li said. "Should I put it back?"

"Yeah, you probably should," Po said, but still, he couldn't help geeking out. "You look so cool, though! How does it feel? Do the hinges hinge? Does it smell like rhino? Does it feel like you can take on a thousand warriors and emerge unscathed?"

Li nodded. "Yeah, it's pretty cool." He noticed a pull string on the armor. "Ooh, I wonder what this does. I should pull it."

He pulled the string, and the armor started to expand. Wings, shields, and weapons popped out from every inch of the metal suit. In the end, a battle flag sprouted from the top of the helmet.

Po gasped. "I think I just peed a little."

Li smiled at his son. The two of them turned and

looked at the items in the hall like kids in a candy store.

"Anything else we should try in here, son? Hmm?" Li asked.

Po grinned at him, and the two started playing with everything in sight. They put rat helmets on their fingers and had a thumb war. They jumped on shields belly-first and slid across the smooth floor like they were snow sledding. Po put on the dolphin armor and he and his dad had a mock battle.

Po was having such a good time that he barely noticed when Master Shifu and the Furious Five walked in. But as soon as he did, he froze, mortified.

"I'm going to get you! I'm going to get you!" Li was teasing, playfully head-butting Po with his armored rhino horn.

"Shh, stop!" Po whispered.

"Why? What's wrong?" Li asked.

Po bounded toward his friends, grinning sheepishly. "Guys! Guys! You're never going to guess who just showed up! Not in a million years!"

Li lifted up the front of his helmet, revealing his panda face.

"Your father!" cried Master Shifu and the Furious Five.

"Whoa, how'd you guess that?" Po asked. "Oh, wait a second. Yeah, of course. We look exactly the same. Dad, say hi to my friends, Mantis, Tigress, Monkey, Crane, and Viper. They're kind of my best friends."

Then he pointed to Master Shifu. "And this . . . this is Master Shifu. Legend."

"It is an honor to meet you, Master Panda," Master Shifu said. He looked at Po. "Perhaps your father would care to join us in the Training Hall?" He turned back to Li. "Your son will be teaching the class."

Each member of the Furious Five winced at the thought of Po teaching again.

"Ho-ho!" cried Li, obviously impressed.

Po thought quickly. The last thing he wanted was for his dad to see what a terrible teacher he was.

"I'm sure he's tired," Po said. "I'm going to show

him to the Chrysanthemum Suite."

Po grabbed his dad by the arm and dragged him away.

"What? Tired? No, I'm fine," Li protested. "I would love to watch you teach."

"Trust me," Po said. "It'd be much more fun to watch me—"

Suddenly a warning gong sounded, echoing through the hall.

"—Fight!" Po finished.

"The valley's under attack!" Tigress cried.

She raced off, followed by the rest of the Five and Master Shifu. Po moved to go with them, but Li held him back.

"Son? Under attack?" he asked worriedly.

"This is perfect!" said Po. "Now you can see what being the Dragon Warrior is all about. Follow me!"

CHAPTER 6
Jombies Attack!

When Po and Li reached the village, Master Shifu and the Furious Five were on the rooftops, already locked in battle. Their opponents were green and glowing. They didn't know it yet, but they were facing Kai's jade creatures, the kung fu masters now under the evil yak's control.

Po leaped through the air.

"Enemies of justice! Prepare for—" Po began, but the sight of the glowing Jade Zombies broke his focus. He botched his landing and fell hard onto the rooftop. "What's the deal with the green guys?" he asked, shaking off the fall.

Tigress punched one of the warriors and grimaced. It was like hitting solid rock.

"Argh!" she cried. "Some kind of Jade Zombies."

Monkey landed near Po.

"Jade Zombies?" Po repeated.

Then he and Monkey had the same thought at the same time.

"Jombies!" they yelled together. "Jinx!"

Li rushed up, panting, and called up to the rooftop. "Lotus! Be careful!"

"It's okay, Dad! I do this every—"

A green warrior lunged at him, and Po fended off the blow with a swift movement of his hands. A second warrior, identical to the first, attacked him on his other side.

"Whoa. I recognize these guys!" Po cried. "The Master Badger Twins! With their Crushing Double Gong Technique!"

The two jombie badgers crashed into him from either side, hitting him square in the head.

"Yeah, that's the one!" Po yelled, pushing them both away. Then he noticed something else strange. "That guy is . . . Noooo! Master Porcupine!"

The spiky jombie launched one of his sharp darts at Po, and Monkey flew in to deflect it.

"I thought he died a hundred years ago," Monkey said. He threw the dart back at the porcupine, and it smashed into bits on contact.

"These guys are legend!" Po said excitedly.

He reached down from the roof and plucked the village sketch artist from the crowd.

"Get a quick sketch of us!" he said, as he hurled himself back into the battle.

The little pig quickly sketched Po, who smiled and posed between delivering punches.

"Did you get it? Did you get it?" Po asked. He rushed over to the pig and looked at the sketch. "Aw, I blinked! Can we get another one?"

Whoosh! Master Porcupine hurled himself at Po, and they both tumbled over the roof. They crashed through the ceiling of the back room of the noodle shop, Po's old bedroom. The jombie wrapped his hands around Po's neck as they fell.

"I'm being choked by Master Porcupine! This is so cool!" Po said. He grabbed his Master Porcupine action figure off his shelf. "Look! It's you!"

Master Shifu jumped into the room and knocked Master Porcupine off Po.

"Po, focus!" he warned.

Po went flying backward and crashed through the floor and down into Mr. Ping's kitchen.

"Sorry, Dad! I'll clean it up later!" Po said, scrambling to his feet as two jombie warriors appeared and attacked him. He grabbed the nearest weapon he could find—a frying pan.

"Whoa, whoa, not my good pan!" cried Mr. Ping. "Take this one!"

He took the pan from Po's hand and replaced it with a soup ladle. Po used it to fight off the warriors as best as he could.

Li ran into the kitchen.

"Watch out!" he yelled, and just in time. One of the jombies was about to deliver a crushing blow to Po's head, and Po ducked it.

Then he got a gleam in his eye.

"Check out my Dumplings of Doom!" he cried, and Viper and Tigress appeared to help.

Po snatched some bowls, soared through the air, and smashed down on a table full of dumplings. As the dumplings shot into the air, Po caught them into the bowls and then poured them into his mouth.

Viper wrapped around Po's belly, and Tigress yanked on Viper, sending the dumplings blasting out of Po's mouth at rocket speed.

Bam! Bam! Bam! The dumplings knocked down the warriors each time they made contact.

Mantis, Crane, and Monkey showed up, and together with Po, the Furious Five pinned the jombies to the floor.

"Gotcha!" Po said.

Suddenly, all of the jade creatures began to speak at once. Kai was speaking through them. He could speak through their mouths and see the battle through their eyes. And what he saw was that Po's green chi glowed brighter and stronger than everyone else's.

"I see you," the jombies said in a spooky voice.

"Your chi will soon be mine."

"Is he talking to me?" Po asked.

"Which one?" asked Tigress. "They're all talking."

"Wow, you're right," said Po. "That's so scary! We should try that too . . . maybe it'd be scary back at them."

"Okay," Mantis agreed. "But we gotta plan what we're gonna say first or else it won't be scary, it'll just be stupid."

"It's not *them* talking, you idiots!" yelled the jombies. "It's me talking through them. Kai!"

"Who?" asked Po and the Furious Five in unison.

Kai frowned. "Okay, okay, enough," he said through the jombies.

Suddenly, the jombies vaporized into green streaks and flew away, up and over the rooftops.

"Whoa! What just happened?" asked Monkey.

"Did you see that?" Po asked. "They just . . . the green smoke just poof . . . and they poof—Shifu, what was that?"

Master Shifu looked thoughtful. "Kai . . . Kai . . . Nope, never heard of him."

CHAPTER 7
Ooqway's Tale

Everyone returned to the Jade Palace, including Mr. Ping and Li. They all gathered in the scroll room as Master Shifu searched the overflowing shelves to find the scroll he was looking for.

"Kai . . . Kai . . . where is it?" Master Shifu muttered. "There's so much wisdom in here, I can't find anything!"

After a few more minutes he let out a triumphant cry.

"Yes!" He pulled a scroll off a high shelf and

jumped down to join the others.

"Behold. All the answers will be found within," he said solemnly.

He unrolled the scroll—and it was blank.

"What? Are you kidding me? Not again!" he fumed. Then he unraveled some more. "Wait, wait. Sorry. Oh, okay, here we go. It is written in Oogway's hand."

They all gathered around as Master Shifu read from the scroll.

> Long ago, I had a brother in arms.
> I was an ambitious young warrior
> leading a great army. And fighting
> by my side was Kai, my closest friend.
>
> One day we were ambushed. I was
> badly wounded. My friend carried me
> for days, looking for help, until we
> came upon a secret village, high in
> the mountains. An ancient place of
> healing.
>
> A village of pandas.

Everyone gasped and looked at Po.

"Pandas?" Po said, looking down to the scroll, where there was a sketch of a group of pandas surrounding Oogway.

Master Shifu continued reading.

Yes! Pandas! The pandas used the power of chi to heal me. They taught me the power to give chi. But Kai wanted the power all to himself. He saw that what could be given could also be taken.

The scroll showed a terrifying image of Kai sucking chi from the one of the pandas.

I had to stop him. Our battle shook the earth. Until, finally, I banished Kai to the Spirit Realm.

Should he ever return to the mortal realm, he can only be stopped by a true Master of Chi.

Everyone stared at Master Shifu.

"Me? I can barely make a flower bloom. I'd need at least thirty more years, and a cave!" Master Shifu protested.

Crane anxiously flapped his wings. "Chi master. We need a chi master."

"He will continue stealing the chi of masters until he has consumed it all," Viper said.

"There is no choice. We fight," Tigress said firmly.

Po looked at the scroll, at the drawing of pandas huddled around Oogway, as the Five continued to talk.

Li looked from Po to Master Shifu, to the Furious Five—their faces frowning as they struggled to come up with a plan. Then Li stepped forward. "I can teach you, son," he said.

Po looked up at his father. "You can do this?"

"Of course," Li replied. "I'm a panda."

"That must be why the universe sent you here!" Po guessed. "Okay, so what do I have to do?"

"You have to come home with me," said Li.

Po's eyes widened. "To the secret village?"

"You must rediscover what it is to be a panda," Li explained. "You have to learn how to live like a panda. Sleep like a panda. Eat like a panda. Those hundred-and-three dumplings? I was just warming up."

Po nodded. "I've always felt like I wasn't eating up to my full potential."

Mr. Ping ran up to Li. "You can't take Po away from me! No, no, I want a second opinion. Shifu, open another scroll or something."

"I think he should go," Master Shifu said.

"Fine!" Mr. Ping snapped. "A third opinion! Monkey? Tigress?"

Po interrupted him. "Dad, you heard what Shifu said Oogway said: This guy can only be stopped by a Master of Chi. And I can only master chi by knowing who I really am. Well, I'm a panda."

Mr. Ping frowned. He couldn't argue with that. Po was a panda, and he deserved to be with other pandas, even if it broke Mr. Ping's own noodle-loving heart.

"I'll pack you a lunch for the road," he said.

Li and Po set out for the village at sunrise the next morning. The Furious Five and Master Shifu stood at the top of the Jade Palace steps and watched them go.

"Do you really think Po can master chi in time?" Viper asked.

"It doesn't matter what I think," Master Shifu responded. "It matters only what the universe thinks."

"So that's a no?" Mantis piped up.

Crane looked worried. "Master, what are we going to do?"

"You are going to find out where Kai is," Master Shifu replied. "Follow the trail of those jade creatures. But do not engage, for with every foe he faces, Kai becomes stronger."

"Why me? Is it because I asked?" Crane wondered.

"No," said Master Shifu. "It is because you can fly. Go!"

Crane gulped and put on his flat straw hat. Mantis jumped on the brim.

"Should've kept your beak shut," he told his friend.

"And take Mantis," Master Shifu added.

"What?" Mantis complained. "Oh man. Is it because I—"

"Yes," said Master Shifu.

So with Mantis perched on his hat, Crane flew off to find Kai . . . and certain danger.

CHAPTER 8
Journey to the Secret Panda Village

It was a long way to the Panda Village. Po and Li left the Valley of Peace far behind and walked until they reached a range of snowy mountains. Then they began to climb higher and higher.

Grrooooowl! Po's stomach rumbled from hunger.

"Lunch break?" asked Li.

"You don't need to ask me twice," Po said. He set down his travel sack.

"*Ow!*" came a voice from within.

Po's eyes narrowed. "Dad?"

"Yes?" Li replied, but Po wasn't talking to Li.

Po stared at the sack. "Dad?" he repeated, louder this time, as he opened the sack, revealing Mr. Ping inside.

"Yes?" Mr. Ping answered meekly.

He popped his head out.

"What are you doing?" Po asked.

"What am I doing? Getting a backache!" Mr. Ping complained. "Did you have to step on every rock?"

"No, I mean why are you here?" Po pressed him.

"What was I supposed to do?" Mr. Ping asked. "What if the pandas don't have food you like? You're never going to be able to save the world on an empty stomach. I consider my presence mission critical."

"Well, you know we can't share the location of the village with others!" Li reminded him.

"You think I can't keep a secret?" Mr. Ping shot back. "I raised Po for twenty years before I finally told him he was adopted."

"Seriously?" Li asked.

Po shrugged sheepishly.

Li gave in. "Okay. I guess it would be cruel to make you fly back."

Po stared at Mr. Ping. "You can fly? How come you never taught me?!"

They ate a quick meal and then continued through the mountains. The snow was waist-deep, but Po and Li plodded through it. Mr. Ping's webbed feet allowed him to walk lightly across the surface.

"We're here," Li announced suddenly.

They had come to a stop in front of a towering wall of ice, its top lost in the snow swirling high overhead.

"Sure looks like a long way up there," Mr. Ping said. "And my son hates stairs. So let's go home."

"We're pandas," Li said simply. He pulled a hidden rope and a wicker basket appeared in the snow below them.

Li grinned. "We don't do stairs."

Po's face lit up with joy. "I've waited my whole life to hear those words!"

"Rats!" said Mr. Ping.

They all climbed into the basket and Li tugged on the ropes. They were pulled up the side of the ice wall, higher and higher.

They rose above the clouds, and the basket stopped moving. As the mist around them parted, Po could see . . . more mist.

"Huh?" Po wondered.

"This is the secret Panda Village?" Mr. Ping asked. "No wonder you keep it a secret. If I lived here, I wouldn't tell anyone either."

They climbed out of the basket. Boards creaked under Po's foot as he stepped out. Were they on some kind of bridge?

Li, Po, and Mr. Ping walked forward, passing underneath an arch.

"Now you can 'whoa'," he said.

The fog cleared, and Po's eyes widened as he tried to take in the sight before him. The village was nestled among towering snowy mountains, but the village itself was lush and green. A bubbling stream ran through a bamboo forest, and crystal blue water cascaded down a waterfall.

But what stunned Po the most were the pandas. There were so many of them! Adorable panda kids ran through the village, laughing and flying kites. Other pandas snoozed peacefully in hammocks, or played mah-jongg in the shade, or relaxed in steaming thermal pools.

One by one, the pandas noticed Li, Po, and Mr. Ping.

"Li's back!" a panda shouted.

"He's found his son!" another added.

The pandas let out a cheer and began to run across the green fields toward Po and Li. Then they all stopped to catch their breath. In a minute they were running toward him again.

"Why are we running?" asked a slightly confused, bigger panda.

Soon Po was surrounded by dozens of pandas. Cute baby pandas stared at him shyly from the safety of their parents' legs. Po smiled and gave them a friendly wave.

"Everyone! Gather around! This is my son!" Li called out proudly.

The pandas swarmed Po, hugging him and shaking his hand.

"Easy, easy!" Li laughed.

A panda with graying fur stepped forward.

"This is Grandma Panda, our village elder," Li said.

Grandma Panda looked Po up and down. "Hmm, he's so handsome," she said. "Just like his father."

"Thank you!" Mr. Ping said proudly.

Li turned to two massive pandas standing next to him, both wearing eager expressions.

"Son, these are your cousins, Dim and Sum."

"I have cousins!" Po said excitedly.

Dim hung a lei made of dumplings around Po's neck.

"Welcome!" he said.

Po looked at the dumpling lei admiringly. "Whoa, buns on a string."

"We call it a snacklace," said Sum.

But just as Po was about to take a bite, a bunch of pandas swarmed him. At first Po thought they were coming in for a group hug, until he heard munching noises. When they backed away, the snacklace was just a string.

Sum shrugged. "We'll make you another one."

The slightly confused panda, whom Po learned was named Big Fun, was now teary-eyed. "It's you!" he cried, squeezing Po in a tight panda bear hug.

"Oh, that's nice," Po managed to squeak out. "Hi."

"I don't know who you are," Big Fun said warmly.

A baby panda named Lei Lei reached into Po's pocket and pulled out a Tigress action figure.

"Oooh, Stripy Baby! So beautiful!" she said, clapping her hands.

"Okay, careful with that," Po said, reaching out to grab it back.

Lei Lei looked at Po with her wide baby eyes. "Can I keep her?" she asked, hugging the Tigress action figure close.

Po couldn't refuse. "No . . . problem," he said. "Of course. That's why I brought her. Take good care of her?"

"Yay! Stripy Baby!" she cried happily.

As Po looked at Lei Lei, something struck him.

"You're just like me, but a baby!" he said.

He looked at Grandma Panda.

"You're like me, but old!" he cried.

Grandma Panda grinned.

He turned to Dim and Sum. "You're like me . . . but fatter!"

Dim and Sum high-fived him.

Po gazed out at all the pandas, at all the furry faces and big bellies and tiny ears and black noses.

"You *all* look like me," he said softly.

A strange feeling welled up inside Po, one he had never felt before. All his life he had been surrounded by pigs and bunnies and geese. He'd battled alongside a tiger, a monkey, a praying mantis, a crane, and a snake. He'd battled rhinos, gorillas, a leopard, and even a peacock. And always, wherever he went, he had been the only big-bellied, furry, black-and-white guy in sight.

For the first time in his life, he fit in.

"Let's feast in my son's honor," Li said, motioning

downhill. The pandas began flopping to the ground and rolling.

Po was confused. "What the—?"

Dim and Sum plopped down on the ground. They rolled down the hill like furry balls.

"Pandas don't walk, we roll!" Li explained, waving to Po.

Soon every panda in the village was rolling down the hill, expertly dodging logs and rocks on the way down. They all ended up in one big, furry heap at the bottom of the hill.

Mr. Ping shook his head. "Have you ever seen anyone look so ridiculous?" he scoffed.

Beside him, Po plopped onto the grass.

"Po, what are you doing? Po!" Mr. Ping yelled.

Po paused. As the Dragon Warrior, he had jumped, leaped, bounded, raced, zoomed, and flipped—but rolling was a new thing.

Then he launched himself down the hill, rolling after his new panda family.

CHAPTER 9
Panda Party!

Po wobbled a little bit as he rolled, he hit every obstacle in his path, and he crashed into the banquet table instead of the furry panda pile—but he did it!

Po stood up. "You're right, that is better than walking."

The pandas cheered. As they headed to the banquet, a little boy named Bao walked up to Po.

"What kind of panda doesn't know how to roll?" he asked suspiciously.

"Well, I'm kinda new at this whole being-a-panda thing," Po replied.

The kid turned to Mr. Ping. "And what kind of panda are you?"

"I'm not a panda at all."

"What's that?" Bao asked, gesturing to Mr. Ping's head.

Mr. Ping shrugged. "My hat."

Bao gestured to his face. "What's that?"

"My beak," Mr. Ping replied. Bao was just starting another question when Mr. Ping shouted, "No more questions!"

All the pandas dug into the food piled high on the table, grabbing it with their hands.

"Here, son, I packed your chopsticks!" Mr. Ping said, shoving the tools into Po's hand.

"Thanks, Dad!" Po said.

The other pandas stopped eating and looked at him quizzically.

"What?" Po asked.

"What are those for?" asked Bao.

"These? These are chopsticks," Po replied.

"They're for picking up dumplings."

To demonstrate, Po picked up a dumpling between the two sticks.

Bao looked surprised. "You mean, you only eat one at a time?"

He picked up a mound of dumplings with his hands and shoved them into his mouth, all at once! As Po looked around the table, he realized that all the pandas were eating that way.

He looked down at his hands. One held the chopsticks and a single dumpling, and the other was empty. He gasped.

"I knew I wasn't eating up to my potential!"

Po grabbed the dumpling out of his chopsticks, tossed them aside, and grabbed a second dumpling with his other hand. Then he shoved them both into his mouth at the same time!

Now it was Mr. Ping's turn to gasp. He was horrified! But everyone else cheered.

Suddenly a gong sounded through the village. Everyone stopped eating and turned toward an empty stage just beyond the banquet table.

On the stage, four umbrellas were twirling in unison. A beautiful panda walked through them, her face covered by a fan. Po dropped his dumpling.

"I am Mei Mei," said the panda, locking eyes with Po from behind her fan.

"Wow! She's amazing! She's so beautiful!" Mei Mei said, faking Po's voice from behind her fan.

She switched back to her regular voice and batted her long eyelashes. "That's sweet, Po. But please try to save all other compliments until after the performance."

"Me?" Po said, looking confused. "No, I didn't say—"

"Shh, shh, shut it," Mei Mei hushed him. "After the performance."

From his seat, Mr. Ping rolled his eyes. "Has it started yet?"

Mei Mei unfurled a ribbon from each hand and twirled them expertly. With a *snap!* she whipped a flute into the hands of a nearby panda, and then a cymbal to another. They started playing, and she began to dance around the stage.

Li elbowed Po. "Best ribbon dancer in the world. At least, that's what she says."

Mei Mei's eyes met Po's as she danced. "Look away," she said. "You can't, can you?"

Po turned back to Li. "Dad, why does she keep staring at me like that?"

"Try to keep up," Mei Mei said with a wink. She then wrapped Po in her ribbon, yanking him out of his seat.

"Heh, I, uh, don't really know how to dance," Po said.

"Of course you do! All pandas dance!" said Mei Mei. She reeled Po in closer and dipped him. "I know what you're thinking."

"You do?"

"How can one panda be so beautiful?"

Po laughed nervously as Mei Mei whipped him in the other direction. Using her ribbons like puppet strings, she made Po grab some flowers from offstage and give them to her.

"For me?!" she said, puppeting Po again to kiss her hand.

"Help me, Dads!" Po shouted to Li and Mr. Ping as Mei Mei twirled him past them.

"Yeah, no. You're on your own." Li laughed as Mei Mei reeled him in again.

"You're doing great, son!" Mr. Ping shouted encouragingly.

"Your turn!" Mei Mei said, handing Po a ribbon.

But Po wasn't the most graceful ribbon dancer— he yanked a cymbal out of the hands of the musician and hit himself in the face! Then his feet got tangled in the ribbon and he toppled over with a *thud*.

Mei Mei used her ribbons to yank him back onto his feet before holding him above her head in a final pose. The crowd went wild—even Mr. Ping couldn't help but cheer.

As Mei Mei flung Po back into his seat, Li leaned over to him. "Don't worry, you'll get the hang of it."

"I have so much to learn," Po said. But as the pandas of the village surrounded him, the road ahead felt a little easier. After all, he had loads of good teachers to help him.

CHAPTER 10
Fear the Bug!

While Po and Mr. Ping were in the Panda Village, Mantis and Crane continued their search for Kai and the jombies.

Mantis rode on top of Crane's hat as they soared over a desert stretching for miles in every direction.

"Wings of Surveillance!" Crane called out, like it was a special kung fu move.

"Why do you do that?" Mantis complained.

"Do what?" Crane asked.

"Just because you say 'Wings of . . .' before

something doesn't mean that you're doing a special move. It's like me saying, 'Antenna of Power.' Or 'Thorax of Making Sandwiches.'"

Crane looked up at his friend. "Wings of Disagreement."

"Whoa! There!" Mantis cried suddenly, pointing down below.

Three kung fu masters were making their way across the desert: Master Bear, Master Croc, and Master Chicken. Crane swooped down toward them.

"*Cluck!* Jade creatures attacked our villages! We've tracked them here," Master Chicken said.

"Stop!" Master Bear boomed.

The group froze. They had arrived at an old, abandoned ship in the middle of the desert. A gaping hole opened up into the hull.

"They must be in there," Master Bear said.

Crane frowned. He and Mantis were supposed to be on a scouting mission, not an attacking one. Kai was just too dangerous.

"Master Shifu strongly advises—" Crane began,

but Master Bear raised his giant battle-axes and ran toward the ship with a mighty cry.

"Yaaaaaaaaargh!"

Master Croc followed him.

"Ooooh waaaaah!"

"—not to engage," Crane finished, but it was too late.

"We've got to get in there," Mantis urged him.

"Master Shifu said—" Crane repeated.

"You're seriously afraid?" Mantis asked. "Even Master Chicken is going in. And he's a chicken."

Master Chicken's feathered tail disappeared through the hole in the ship as he followed his friends. Seconds later a bright green light flashed. The screams of the three kung fu masters rang through the desert.

"That's it, I'm going in!" Mantis said, preparing to jump off Crane's hat.

Crane didn't like this one bit. "Mantis! We have orders not to—"

"They need our help," Mantis interrupted him. "Come on, I'll go high, you go low!"

KUNG FU PANDA 3

Mantis leaped up and entered the ship through a small crack in the wood. Crane sighed. It was one thing to leave the other masters behind. But Mantis was his friend.

"Fear the bug!" Crane heard Mantis yell from inside the ship. "All right you little . . . uh-oh."

Crane didn't hesitate. "Hold on, buddy. I'm coming!" he cried, flying toward the ship. He could still hear Mantis.

"Antenna of Power! Ah, it didn't work!"

A large crash came from inside the ship. Then another green light flashed.

"Mantis!" Crane yelled.

He dove inside the ship and landed, his wings ready to deliver kung fu punishment to the first Jade Zombie he saw. He slowly crept into the darkness.

"Mantis?" he called out softly. "Mantis?"

The silence inside the ship was eerie. Crane felt the feathers on the back of his neck prickle. Slowly, he turned . . .

. . . and found himself looking up at a big, green glowing yak warrior! Crane knew it must be Kai.

KUNG FU PANDA 3

69

Crane whistled a nervous tune and lowered his hat, but when he tried to walk away casually, Kai lunged. Crane flew up over Kai's head, delivering a kung fu kick to Kai as he moved.

"Your chi is strong," Kai remarked. "Just like your friend, the bug."

With a smug grin, he put a hand on his belt to show Crane the new amulets that dangled there— Master Bear, Master Croc, Master Chicken, and Mantis.

"Mantis!" Crane cried.

Kai took advantage of Crane's moment of weakness. He jumped in the air and pushed his right hand forward, sending a wave of pure chi energy at Crane. The powerful force slammed him against a wall and left him gasping with shock.

"Don't worry, little birdie," Kai said. "I'll put your chi to good use—destroying the Jade Palace and everyone in it."

"No!" Crane yelled. He grabbed the nearest object—a wooden keg—and hurled it at Kai. Then he soared up, crashing through the deck of the boat.

Kai launched his chain blades at Crane. They wrapped around Crane's feet and wings.

"Wings of . . . Regret!" Crane said.

Kai yanked Crane back into the boat. Kai's eyes glowed green with chi—but also with greed.

CHAPTER 11
Panda Training

Po had no idea the danger that his friends were in. But he knew he had one main purpose in the Panda Village—to learn how to harness his panda nature so he could become a Master of Chi.

Po jumped out of bed bright and early the next morning and went over to the little flowerpot in his hut. Inside it was a little wilted flower.

"Oh yeah. First day of panda training. All right, flower, I'm gonna make you bloom!" he cried.

He ran outside and across a bridge to Li's hut.

His father was still sleeping, snoring peacefully in a big, comfy bed.

"Dad," Po said, but Li didn't stir. "Dad!"

Li sat up, startled.

"What? What is it?"

"I'm ready for my first day of panda training!" Po announced. He was practically bouncing off the walls with energy.

"Well, pandas sleep past noon," Li grumbled. "So lesson number one is . . . go back to bed!"

Po headed back to his hut, shaking his head. "Of course," he scolded himself.

Po fluffed up his pillow and straightened his blanket. "Nobody said this was going to be easy."

Then he climbed into bed—and fell asleep instantly.

Before Po knew it, Li burst into his hut. Po shot upright.

"Did I oversleep?" he asked.

"You sure did!" Li replied proudly.

"Yes!" Po cheered.

Li brought Po into the village, where a bunch of

young pandas were lined up, eager to help Po.

Some of the pandas started passing a little puck with feathers called a jianzi back and forth, kicking it or batting it away. The jianzi flew toward Po and he joined in.

Bao did a bunch of cool moves, egging Po on. "Can you do this? Can you do that?" he said, kicking it forward and under the knee.

Finally Bao kicked the jianzi to Po. He caught it with his foot and kicked it high in the air. It soared across the field, up to the top of the hill. Po could see Grandma Panda standing there.

"Uh-oh, Grandma Panda, heads up!" Po yelled.

"Hello!" she called. Then, "D'oh!" The jianzi nailed her on the head, knocking her down.

"We better roll," Li said, and they all quickly rolled off.

Po was grateful that it was time for rolling practice. He, Li, and the young pandas lined up on top of the hill when Po spotted Mr. Ping halfway down, holding a big bowl of noodles.

"Po, lunchtime!" he called up to his son.

Po had already started rolling down the hill with the other pandas.

"Ah!" cried Mr. Ping as he darted between the rolling pandas.

Po continued to hurl himself down the hill, once again hitting every rock and tree in his path. When he reached the bottom, he crashed on top of Li.

Li shook his head. "You gotta let the hill tell *you* where to roll."

"Rookie mistake," Po said as he started to walk back up the hill.

Li stopped Po before he went any farther. Then he walked over to Dim and Sum, who were standing next to two bamboo trees with a hammock hung between them.

"Dim, Sum, let's show him how we go uphill," Li instructed.

Dim and Sum backed up into the hammock, and then Li pulled back on the trees and released.

Boing! The hammock launched them into the air! They flew all the way up the hill and landed in the grass.

"Whoooooooo!" they cheered as they flew.

Po watched them admiringly. "It's beautiful."

Po ran to the catapult and copied what his cousins had done. He went flying up the hill, over Mr. Ping's head.

Still trying to entice Po, Mr. Ping had whipped up some crispy tofu for a snack.

"Snack time!" he called out cheerfully. Then he noticed Po, airborne above him.

"I may never walk again!" Po crowed.

"That's what I'm afraid of!" said Mr. Ping.

Po crashed into his cousins, who had landed perfectly, as they were splayed out in lounge chairs on top of the hill. Mr. Ping winced. He shook his head as Po rolled down another hill.

"Just let yourself fall into it," Li instructed Po, who was back at the top of the hill again.

Po took a deep breath and tried to relax as best as he could. Then he closed his eyes and tried to roll . . . but instead he fell backward, headfirst into a rock! And then another . . . and another.

Eventually he rolled right into Mei Mei, who

was practicing her ribbon dancing. The two ended up tangled together in the ribbons.

"Subtle, Po," Mei Mei said, locking eyes with him. "Very subtle."

Po blushed.

"Let me get some of that," said Big Fun, who ran over and picked both of them up in a huge hug.

Once he managed to free himself, Po catapulted himself back uphill to try again.

This time as Po rolled, he picked up speed and snow, turning into a panda snowball. But Po couldn't see where he was going!

"What are you guys looking at?" one of the pandas asked as he walked past Li and the others at the bottom of the hill, a chair and umbrella in hand.

BOOM! Po collided with him. Snow exploded everywhere and Po went flying into the nearby hot spring.

"Yaaaa hoooooo!" Po shouted, landing perfectly in the pool chair. The umbrella opened right above him.

Li laughed, beaming a proud smile. "That's how

we roll! Cannonball!" he cried, jumping into the spring.

The other pandas cheered and followed him into the water—even Grandma Panda on her bamboo raft!

Meanwhile, Mr. Ping was sad as he returned to the village cooking hut. He had been working so hard, making all of Po's favorite dishes, but Po wasn't even interested! Po *never* said no to his dumplings. *Never!*

Ever since Li had come to the Valley of Peace, Mr. Ping had worried that he would lose Po. Now it looked like that might happen. Mr. Ping would be left all alone. No more Po. No more cuddly panda son.

When he entered the hut, his eyes grew wide. He had prepared a whole feast for Po—radish noodles, tofu noodles, scallion noodles—and the table was crawling with pandas! Bao, Lei Lei, and the baby pandas were eating everything in sight.

"What are you doing here?" Mr. Ping asked. "That food is for Po!"

He rushed around the hut, trying to shoo away the baby pandas. One was shoveling dumplings into his mouth from a big bowl. Another was reaching a curious hand toward the cooking fire, and Mr. Ping scooped him up under a wing and whisked him away.

Bao tossed a baby panda into a pot. "Throw it in!" he cried.

"Get out of there! No!" Mr. Ping shouted.

Then he noticed a bowl of noodles rapidly disappearing. His leg got wrapped around the long noodle from the bowl. It dragged him all around the hut, winding around all the baby pandas.

"Ah, my noodles! Leave my noodles alone!"

He finally managed to grab the noodle and stop it. With another hand he grabbed his hat. He didn't realize that it was inside a baby panda's mouth.

"No, no, no, not for you!" Mr. Ping scolded.

The panda opened his mouth and the hat shot out, slamming into Mr. Ping. He went flying across the hut—and landed next to Bao, who was slurping up the long noodle.

"We love noodles!" said Bao.

Mr. Ping gasped. "Just like my Po!"

Suddenly he softened. He saw all the young pandas in a new light. Maybe he would lose Po, and maybe he wouldn't. But right now, he had lots of baby pandas to feed. Just like the old days, but with more pandas!

Oh, what the heck? Mr. Ping thought as he put out more food.

All the little pandas started munching away, and Mr. Ping smiled for the first time in days.

CHAPTER 12
Is This My Mom?

That night Po and Li sat on the porch of Li's hut, looking out at the village below them. Po gave a deep, contented sigh.

"How was that?" he asked Li, because sighing contentedly was another panda skill he needed to perfect.

Li held up a finger and then took a deep breath, letting out an even bigger, deeper, more contented sigh than Po's.

Po was impressed. "Whoa!"

"Now, you try again," said Li. "But don't try so hard."

Po nodded and tried again, finally getting it. It wasn't about how much air you took in or let out. It was about how you felt when you did it.

One more time, he sighed. This one was almost as deep and contented as Li's had been.

"Much better," Li said.

Po pumped his fist victoriously. "Yes! Thanks, Dad."

"For what?" Li asked.

"You know," said Po. "For showing me what it feels like . . . to be a panda. So when do you think I'll be ready to master chi?"

"Soon. Real soon. Come on," Li said. He started to stand up. "I want to show you something else."

Po followed Li inside his hut. The floor was strewn with dirty clothes.

"Sorry about the mess," Li apologized. "I don't usually get visitors."

They stepped around the clothes until they reached the front of a small shrine on the far wall.

In the center of the shrine was a picture surrounded by lit candles and flowers—a picture of baby Po in the arms of a female panda.

"Is this my mom?" Po asked.

"I had this done on your one hundredth day," Li told him, picking up the picture. "Your momma couldn't hold you still. You nearly ate the paper. It's true."

Po saw that a corner of the sketch had actually been nibbled on.

"What was she like?" Po asked.

"She was the total package," Li responded, with a far-off look in his eyes. "Smart. Beautiful. Tremendous appetite. She was the love of my life. And then, just when I thought I couldn't get any luckier, along you came."

He glanced over at Po and smiled.

"I really had it all," he said. Then his face clouded. "Until that one moment when I lost everything. . . ." His voice trailed off.

Even though Po had been just a baby at the time, he remembered that moment. He dreamed about it, sometimes. The evil Lord Shen had sent his army of wolves to attack Po's peaceful farming village, far from the safety of the secret village. Li stayed to fight, and told Po's mother to take Po to safety. She ran and hid Po in a crate of vegetables. Po was found and adopted by Mr. Ping, and his mother . . . his mother was lost forever.

Li's hand trembled as he carefully placed the picture back on the altar. Po saw how heartbroken his father was, and his own heart broke for Li.

Po stepped closer to his father and put a hand on his shoulder.

"Dad. You don't ever have to worry about losing me again," Po promised. He pulled his father into a hug. Li wrapped his arms around Po, squeezing him as tightly as he could.

Suddenly Big Fun ran into Li's hut. "Let me get some of that," he said, picking both of them up into a gigantic hug.

CHAPTER 13
Valley of War

Back at the Jade Palace, Master Shifu, Tigress, Viper, and Monkey stood in the garden of statues, looking out over the valley. Crane and Mantis had not returned, and they were worried.

Even more worrisome were all the messages they were receiving from throughout China. Another one flew in, attached to an arrow. Monkey jumped in the air and grabbed it. He landed next to the others, removed a red piece of parchment, and read it.

"It's from the Eastern Province," Monkey reported.

Master Shifu took the arrow from him and set it in line with the other arrows they had received.

"Master Lizard, Master Ox, Master Eagle . . . all of them. In every village from the sea to here. Every master in China has vanished," he said.

"Maybe they are all at a party?" Monkey suggested hopefully.

Tigress and Viper looked at Monkey.

"Monkey," Viper said in a disapproving voice.

Monkey shrugged. "I didn't get invited either."

But they all knew the truth—even Monkey.

"Kai has taken their chi," Master Shifu said. "We are all that stand between him and the knowledge Oogway left in our care."

He looked at Tigress. "The villagers, evacuated?"

"Done, Master," she replied.

Master Shifu paced around the garden. "Crane? Mantis?"

"Still nothing," Tigress reported.

Then Viper cried out, "Wait! It's them!"

They could see the silhouette of Crane high in the sky, with the tiny Mantis perched on his back.

But as the warriors got closer, they saw that they were both green and glowing.

Master Shifu's heart sank. "No . . ."

Jade Crane dive-bombed them, and the four warriors ducked just in time to avoid him.

Jade Mantis leaped off Jade Crane's back and they both landed in the middle of the statue garden. Behind them, through the smoke, Kai himself appeared. He marched forward past the two jombies.

Master Shifu's eyes narrowed. "Kai."

Kai's entire body was glowing with incredible chi as he looked up at Oogway's statue. Master Shifu and the rest of the Furious Five blocked his path.

"Nice. Very tacky," Kai remarked.

"How dare you set foot on these grounds!" Master Shifu said angrily.

Kai snorted. "Look at you pathetic fools. Groveling at the feet of Oogway."

"You are not fit to speak his name," Tigress said, her eyes like two burning coals as she glared at him.

"I am not fit, little kitten?" Kai asked. "I fought

by his side. I loved him like a brother. And he betrayed me. Well now I will destroy everything he has created!"

He hurled his chain blades at them.

"Go!" Master Shifu yelled.

Monkey, Viper, and Tigress jumped out of the way just in time. Kai's chains whipped like huge, angry snakes with minds of their own. Monkey jumped and leaped over the chains. Viper moved so quickly she was a flash in the air.

Tigress bounded at Kai, delivering a brutal blow that knocked him to the ground.

"How's that for a little kitten?" she asked.

Kai's eyes glowed green with rage. Behind him, Jade Crane and Jade Mantis jumped into the battle.

Jade Crane flew into Tigress, knocking her off Kai. Master Shifu jumped in and unleashed a furious attack.

"I will not let you destroy Oogway's memory!" he yelled.

"Why not?" Kai asked, blocking a blow from Master Shifu. "He destroyed mine."

While Master Shifu and Kai battled, Monkey managed to catch Jade Mantis in his hands.

"Mantis! It is me! Your bestie!" Monkey said.

But Jade Mantis was completely under Kai's control. He used his amazing kung fu strength to fling Monkey back and forth, pummeling Tigress.

"Sorry, Tigress!" Monkey apologized as the two collided. And then they collided again. "Sorry!" And again. "Sorry!"

Master Shifu jumped up to deliver a right heel kick to Kai—and then froze in midair.

He had spotted the Oogway amulet around Kai's neck.

Kai used the moment of weakness to send Master Shifu flying into a stone wall. Tigress ran after him.

Kai held out his hand, pointing at Jade Crane and Jade Mantis.

"Bring them to me!" he commanded.

Jade Crane dragged Viper behind him, and Jade Mantis dragged Monkey. Neither of them could escape from the grasp of the jade masters.

Tigress and Master Shifu watched in horror as Kai sucked the chi from Viper and Monkey. They both shrank and turned into jade amulets!

Tigress moved to attack Kai, but Master Shifu held her back.

"No! You must warn Po!" he told her.

Kai lashed his chains around the Oogway statue, sending Tigress and Master Shifu flying backward.

"I will show you the true power of chi, brother!" he said. "Ye-aaaaaaaaah!"

With a mighty pull, he ripped the statue from the ground.

"No!" Master Shifu cried.

Kai swung the statue around and smashed it right through the Jade Palace, carving through the scroll room. Then he let go. Oogway's statue flew off the mountain, and the scrolls—centuries of wisdom—were scattered by the wind. The statue fell from the steps, shattering in the valley below.

Master Shifu sank to his knees in despair. So much knowledge . . . lost.

"Oogway, forgive me," he said.

The sound of Kai's mocking laughter made him look up.

Kai grabbed Oogway's amulet. "Hmm . . . what do you say, Oogway? Do you forgive him?"

"You may have destroyed the Jade Palace, but you will never succeed," Master Shifu said. "There will always be someone to stop you."

"Who, the panda?" Kai asked. "His chi is strong, but it won't be enough. He will meet the same fate as you—"

"No!" Master Shifu cried.

"—and so will every panda in that village," Kai said.

Kai shot out his hand, sucking in Master Shifu's chi. Master Shifu shrunk into a jade amulet.

Tigress gasped in horror.

"Po, I hope you're ready," she whispered.

Tigress glanced down to see the scroll with Oogway's story at her feet. What luck! Now she could find Po.

She only hoped she would find him before Kai did.

CHAPTER 14
The Truth Revealed

That night Po looked out at the sea of pandas before him. A huge festival was taking place, and everyone was dancing and celebrating. Po chatted with his new friends contentedly—he finally felt like he was one of them, a true panda.

But as Po made his way through the village, he came upon a wilted flower in the ground. He took a deep breath and tried to use the same chi move he'd seen Shifu do.

Just then Po spotted a familiar figure climbing

over the cliff wall at the edge of the village.

"Tigress?" he called after her. At the sound of Po's voice, the music died down and the pandas gathered round.

Po made his way over to Tigress; she looked exhausted and worried.

"Who is she?" Mei Mei asked Po.

Lei Lei looked from the action figure in her hand to Tigress. Her eyes lit up.

"Big Stripy Baby!" she cried happily.

She ran to Tigress and clung to her leg.

"What are you doing here?" Po asked Tigress.

"Kai attacked the valley," she replied. "He's taken every master in China, including Shifu and the others. It's all gone, Po. Everything. Everyone . . ." Her voice trailed off, and she looked away.

"Everyone?" Po asked.

Tigress nodded. "Everyone," she said, and Po let the weight of that sink in.

All the pandas got quiet. Then Mr. Ping spoke up.

"How's my restaurant?" he asked. The pandas looked at him, horrified. "We'll talk later."

"And now Kai is on his way here," Tigress continued. "He's after you, Po. He's after all pandas."

The shocked pandas gasped.

"How long do we have?" Po asked.

"Not long," Tigress replied. "Please tell me you've mastered chi."

Po turned to Li, who was hurrying through the crowd of pandas, trying to get them in order.

"Here, take the baby," he said, handing off a cub to its parents. Then he picked up another. "Okay, who belongs to this one?"

"Dad, Dad!" Po shouted, catching up to him. "You need to teach me the secret chi technique now," he said urgently.

Li had a funny, nervous look on his face. "No, no, I'm afraid you need more time," he said.

He quickly shouted to the pandas. "Everyone, go get your things!" Then he rushed over to a smaller groups of pandas, directing them to get all the food together. "Let me hand you that—"

"I don't have more time," Po argued. "I need to learn it now."

Li grabbed a bowl of food from the table. "Sorry. You're not ready," he said flatly. "Pack everything!" he called to the pandas who were already fleeing into their huts.

"I am ready," Po said.

"Not quite," Li said. Ignoring Po, he headed toward the bridge leading to his hut.

Po wasn't sure why his dad was acting this way.

"What are you talking about?" he questioned him. "I've done everything you've asked. I've mastered napping, sleeping in, hammocks, hot tubs. I am totally at one with my panda parts. Now why won't you show me?"

Li continued to ignore Po and kept walking. Po grabbed Li's arm, forcing his dad to face him.

Li gave in. "Because I don't know it!" he blurted out.

Po was confused. "You what?"

"I don't know it, okay?" Li admitted. "No one does! Maybe we used to . . . but not anymore."

Po was stunned. "You lied?"

"No, I . . . Yes," said Li, looking down.

"Why?" Po asked.

"To save your life!" he cried. "I find out some blade-swinging maniac is coming for you, and I'm supposed to do what—just let that happen?"

"Yes!" Po said. "I'm the Dragon Warrior. Facing maniacs—that's my job. But because of you I left the valley unprotected. I left my friends unprotected. And now they're all . . . they're all . . ." He couldn't say the words. Just thinking of Master Shifu, Viper, Crane, Mantis, and Monkey as little green amulets . . . it was too horrible.

"That would have happened to you, too!" said Li. "I already lost you once. I am not going to lose you again. I can't."

He tried to pull Po toward the hut, but Po pushed him away.

"You just did," he said.

Po walked away from his dad, and Li stared after him, heartbroken.

CHAPTER 15
A New Plan

Li's orders to evacuate the village had sent the pandas into a panic. They scurried back and forth, not sure of what to pack or where to go. Po walked through them, determined. Mr. Ping trailed after him.

"Po, I'm so worried for you that I can't even enjoy being right about everything," Mr. Ping said. "Now run, run, run, as fast as those chubby legs can go!"

"Run?" Po snorted. "There's nowhere to run."

Mr. Ping knew that stubborn look in his son's eyes. "What're you gonna do?"

"I'm gonna stay. And fight that monster."

"Po, he may be a monster, but he's still your father," Mr. Ping said.

"Not him. Kai!"

Po pushed past his dad and rushed to the bamboo forest, kicking and punching, breaking the bamboo to bits. He used the broken parts to piece together a training dummy shaped like Kai.

Po went into his old training routine—dodging, kicking, punching, jumping—but Mr. Ping knew this wasn't the way.

He left Po and went to Li's hut, where he found Li staring at a picture of his wife holding baby Po.

"Hungry?" Mr. Ping asked, holding out a bowl of dumplings.

"Not really," Li said.

"For later, then," Mr. Ping said. He handed the bowl to Li.

"You know, you weren't the only one who was lying," he said.

Li raised a furry eyebrow. "Oh?"

Mr. Ping took a deep breath. "I didn't really come along because I was worried Po would go hungry. I was worried . . . about you," he confessed.

Li was confused. "Worried that I'd go hungry?"

"No!" Mr. Ping corrected him. "I was worried you'd steal Po from me."

Now Li was shocked. "I'd what?"

Mr. Ping looked away, embarrassed.

"I know. That was crazy," said Mr. Ping. "But I realized having you in Po's life doesn't mean less for me. It means more for Po."

Li thought about this. Mr. Ping was right, but what did it matter now?

"Well I'm *not* in his life," he pointed out. "Not anymore."

"Your son got mad at you. Welcome to parenthood."

"I lied to him. . . . He'll never forgive me."

"I lied to him for twenty years. He still thinks he came from an egg. . . . Sometimes we do the wrong things for the right reasons."

Mr. Ping unfolded a piece of paper, placing it next to the picture of Po and his mom.

"Look, he's hurt, he's confused, and he still has to save the world," Mr. Ping told him. "He needs both his dads."

Mr. Ping turned and walked out, and Li looked back at the paper he had left. It was the sketch of Po, Li, and Mr. Ping from the restaurant.

Po did need them. And he wasn't going to give up on Po.

He just had to hope that Po hadn't totally given up on him.

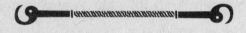

Po was still punching furiously at the training dummy when Tigress blocked his fist midpunch.

"*This* isn't going to work," she said.

"It has to," Po replied, winded.

"You're not thinking straight."

"I am!"

"You're not," she argued back.

As they bickered, they began to spar.

"I've seen Kai. I've seen what he can do," Tigress said, blocking another punch from Po.

"But he hasn't seen what *I* can do," Po said, flipping over. He held Tigress's paw in a familiar pose.

Tigress gasped. "The Wuxi Finger Hold?"

"It's my best move," Po replied. "I just have to get Kai, grab his finger, and then . . . Skadoosh! Back to the Spirit Realm."

Tigress broke his hold. "He has an army of jade creatures. They see everything he sees, so there's no sneaking up on him. You will never get close enough."

"It's gonna work!" Po cried as she dodged a kick from him.

"He can only be stopped by a Master of Chi."

"Oh, you sound just like Shifu with the chi chi chi!" Po shouted, throwing another exhausted punch. "Chi this! Chi that! Chi chi chi chi! I'm *not* a Master of Chi, okay? I don't know if I'm the Dragon Warrior." Po breathed in shakily. "I don't even know if I'm a panda. I don't know *who* I am!" His voice dropped to a whisper, and he collapsed in a heap.

"You're right. There's no way I can stop him."

Li emerged from the fog, breaking the silence. "Unless you had an army of your own."

"You?" Po asked.

"Not just me," Li said.

"Us," said Mr. Ping, by Li's side.

"All of us," Li said. All of the pandas from the village emerged from the fog. "I finally found my son after all these years. It's gonna take a lot more than the end of the world to keep us apart."

Po sighed. "But you don't even know kung fu."

"Then you will teach us," Li said.

"What? I can't teach you kung fu. I couldn't even teach Tigress, and she *already knows* kung fu!"

Li came closer to his son. "Po, I know I'm the last guy you want to trust right now. But you gotta believe me—we can do this. We can learn kung fu. We can be just like you."

Po's eyes lit up. He looked around at all the pandas as an idea started to take hold. "What did you just say?" he asked.

"'We can do this'?" Li ventured.

"No!"

"'We can learn kung fu'?"

"After that!"

"'We can be just like you'?!" Li said, his voice rising.

"Yes!" Po cried.

"We can?"

"No! You *can't*!" Po burst into laughter. The pandas around him thought he'd finally lost it. "But you don't have to be! That's what Shifu meant—I don't have to turn you into *me*. I have to turn you into *you*!"

Mr. Ping shook his head. "That doesn't make any sense."

Po wrapped his two dads in a huge hug. "I know!" Po laughed. "Thanks, Dads!"

"You're welcome?" Ping and Li chorused.

"I'm gonna do something I never thought I'd be able to do: I'm gonna teach kung fu."

CHAPTER 16
Po's Turn to Teach

The next morning Po gathered all of the pandas in a wide field by the waterfall. He had spent all night thinking about his own kung fu training. The field was the perfect location for the exercises he had in mind.

Po put his hands behind his back as he addressed the students. "You guys, your real strength comes from being the best *you* you can be. So who are you? What are you good at? What do you love? What makes you *you*?"

He broke the pandas out into smaller groups. He watched Bao play jianzi, and he studied Mei Mei as she twirled her ribbons. He even watched Big Fun use the hammocks to catapult Dim and Sum up the hills.

Tigress followed him from group to group, but she had no idea what he was doing.

Once Po had figured out what each panda was best at, he had them do it over and over. He asked Bao and all his friends to play a marathon game of jianzi. "Yes, good, good! Again!" he called to them.

He asked another group of pandas to roll downhill, and he had Big Fun practice hugging a log. "Hug that log, you!" he shouted encouragingly. "Hug that log like it's the last time you're ever going to hug it good-bye forever!"

As Mei Mei danced with her ribbons, he called, "Faster, faster! Twirl those ribbons!"

Dim and Sum were off to the side, catapulting themselves with the hammocks. "Higher!" Po said. "And a little more to the left this time—you can do it!"

Then Po took a basket full of dumplings to Bao and the kid pandas. "I don't want to see any of these hit the ground," he coached, before tossing the dumplings into the air.

The kids kicked the dumplings just like they'd kicked the jianzi.

Outside the kitchen hut, Li and Mr. Ping were transforming kitchen supplies into weapons and armor. Tigress walked around, still trying to figure out what Po had in mind. Lei Lei followed her everywhere.

"Wait, wait, Stripy Baby!" she cried.

As Po studied the pandas, he gave them each a different weapon. He handed Mei Mei some nunchucks—two sticks attached by a chain, a weapon used in kung fu fighting. Then he took away her ribbons.

"Good, now try it with these!" he said.

Mei Mei twirled them expertly, though she accidentally hit Tigress in the process.

Then he inserted firecrackers into the dumplings the kids were kicking.

The final test: Po held up a board for each of the pandas to break.

Bao kicked a dumpling clean through the board!

Big Fun hugged the board until it splintered to pieces!

Even Grandma Panda was willing to take a swing at it . . . but she missed and kicked Po in his tenders.

By the end of the day, every panda in the village was turning their own panda skills into awesome battle skills—even though it still looked like they were playing and having fun. Po stood on a hill to watch them all in action. Tigress hobbled over, Lei Lei clinging to her leg.

"They are ready," Po said confidently.

Her golden eyes widened. "What?"

CHAPTER 17
The Battle Begins

After training, Po gathered the pandas at the big banquet table to lay out his battle plan. The pandas looked exhausted but excited as Po used a bamboo stick to point to the details on his plan, which he had drawn on a large scroll.

"Okay, pay attention, 'cause I'm only gonna go over this ten more times," he said. "The only entrance to the village is here."

He pointed to the bridge at the top of the ice wall.

"The Dumpling Squad will take position here."

He slid a bowl of dumplings into place on the map.

"While the Cookie Squad will take position here."

He slid a plate of cookies onto the map.

"Now, on my signal, the two squads will—"

He stopped. The dumplings and cookies were gone! Two little pandas looked innocently at the sky, their cheeks stuffed with food.

Po sighed. "Right, the Noodle Squad will—"

He reached for the noodles, but another panda kid was already slurping them up.

"Well, anyway, the important thing to remember is that THIS is the spot where—"

Crunch! One of the pandas bit the pointer right in half!

Po tossed the pointer aside. "Okay, I saw that coming. If you only remember one thing, it's distract the jombies until I get close enough to put the Wuxi Finger Hold on Kai. Got it?"

"Yeah!" the pandas cheered, and they ran off

to eat dinner. Lei Lei dragged Tigress off in another direction.

Po took out the scroll that Tigress had given him—Oogway's scroll, the scroll that had survived Kai's destruction. That had to mean something.

Po stared at the image of the pandas healing Oogway with their chi.

"I wish I could've taught you this, son," Li said, coming up behind him.

"It's okay, Dad," Po said. He wasn't angry with Li anymore. "I'm—"

Suddenly, the ground started to shake. Startled, the pandas all looked up from their dinner plates.

Tigress looked up from her tea party with Lei Lei. "He's here," she said.

And he was. Kai sank his blades into the ice wall and used them like grappling hooks to climb to the top.

Po stood there, waiting for him by the village gate. The two warriors faced each other like gunslingers. Kai laughed maniacally, and the sound bounced across the hills.

"Whoa! That's what I call a dramatic entrance!" Po said.

When Kai looked at Po, he saw a figure glowing with superstrong chi.

"You must be the Dragon Warrior," Kai said.

"And you must be Kai," said Po. "Beast of Vengeance. Maker of Widows."

"Yes! Finally! Thank you!" Kai said, glad that someone had finally heard of him. "Almost makes me want to spare your life."

"You want to spare me? How about you spare me the chitchat?" Po countered. His eyes narrowed. "Let's do this."

Kai began to boast. "I'm going to take your chi, then the chi of every panda in—"

"Chitchat!" Po interrupted him.

"In the—"

"Chitty chitty chat chat!" said Po.

"In the—"

"Chat chat chat!" Po continued.

"In the—"

"Chitchat!"

"Oh, you pudgy little . . ." Kai had had enough. He looked down at the jade amulets on his belt. He removed them and then started to spin his chain blades as Po slowly backed away.

"Round them all up!" he ordered his jombies.

Using his chain as a sling, he flung the green amulets at Po. They landed in front of him, instantly transforming from tiny amulets into green glowing warriors. The last five to transform were Mantis, Crane, Viper, Monkey, and Master Shifu. Po looked at them in horror—nearly all of his friends had been defeated by Kai and turned into jombies.

"Oh no, it's true," Po said. "You guys have all been turned green . . . except for you, Mantis, you were already green."

Behind Po, Dim and Sum were hiding behind some rocks.

"Now?" Dim whispered.

"Wait for the signal," Sum whispered back.

Kai was impatient. He jumped on top of a rock

and pushed his hands forward, sending the jombies storming at Po.

"Here we go!" Po cried. "Incoming!"

He turned and ran straight into the village. The jombies chased him. Jade Crane swooped down, but Po flipped head over heels to dodge the attack.

"Dumpling Squad!" he cried out.

Now Dim and Sum were in their bamboo catapults.

"Ready?" Dim asked his brother.

"Go time!" said Sum.

They launched into the air, with a cry of "Wahooooo!"

Smoosh! They smashed into Jade Crane from either side with their ample bellies.

Kai shook his head in disbelief. "Seriously?"

Po looked behind him and saw Jade Crane fall. But he had plenty more jombies on his tail.

"Sorry, Crane!" he called back.

Jade Croc leaped at Po from behind, snapping at Po with his massive jaws. Po was just inches in front of him.

"Uh-oh," said Po.

As he zoomed past a hut, a panda hand passed down a heavy metal wok to him. Then he jumped up and took off across the roof of another hut.

"Spring Roll Squad! Time for some takeout!" he commanded.

A group of pandas rolled down from a nearby hill.

"Hup!" they replied.

They rolled down the hill and across the rooftop, building speed.

Bam! Bam! Bam! They knocked down three of the jombies chasing Po like bowling balls taking down pins.

"Yeah!" they cheered.

Po called to the rest of the jombies. "Yoo-hoo! Over here, Mr. Jombie!"

They took off after Po as he used the wok to slide down the slanted rooftop. He hopped out of it and then high-fived a panda paw jutting out from a snowbank.

Jade Monkey had the lead in the jombie chase. But before he could reach Po, Big Fun emerged from the snowbank. He wrapped Monkey in a huge hug!

"I don't know who you are!" Big Fun said cheerfully.

The other jombies were hot on Po's heels as he continued to race through the village.

"Noodle Squad!" he yelled.

Red ribbons immediately lashed out and wrapped around the two Jade Badger Twins. Mei Mei pulled the jombies close.

"Get ready to dance . . . with danger!" Mei Mei cried, whipping out her nunchucks.

"Sweet!" Po cheered as he kept running.

Kai didn't like what he was seeing. "Wait? What? No!" he fumed.

As Po continued on, Tigress sprang out and battled Jade Croc. The little panda girl tottered toward her with her arms outstretched

"Stripy Baby!" she cooed happily.

"Uh-oh!" said Tigress. She scooped up Lei Lei in one hand and fought Jade Croc with the other.

Lei Lei reached out and hit Jade Croc on the

nose with her Tigress action figure.

"You're mean! *Hi-yaaaa!*" she cried.

Tigress backed that up with an even harder punch. *"Ya!"*

Po kept running. Now Jade Bear was behind him, raising his axe. Po tumbled out of the way of the blow as . . .

"Fire in the hole!" yelled Bao.

Bang! An explosion lit up near Jade Bear's face, stopping him in his tracks. Bao and the panda kids were kicking fireworks-stuffed dumplings down onto the jombies.

Bang! They took out Jade Porcupine next.

"All right, kids!" Po cheered.

He glanced behind him. The pack of jombies chasing him was dwindling as the pandas did their jobs. They whacked the jombies with nunchucks, crushed them with hugs, and frazzled them with fireworks.

Now one jombie was closing in on Po—Jade Master Shifu.

"Oh no! Master Shifu! I can't hit Master Shifu!" Po cried.

Then . . . *smash!* Jade Master Shifu ran straight into a frying pan.

Mr. Ping, wearing armor made of cooking pots and pans, smiled. "I can!"

"And so can I!" Li added. He was wearing a massive bamboo replica of Master Flying Rhino's battle armor that he'd tried on in the Jade Palace—and Mr. Ping was strapped to his belly!

"Double Dad Defense!" the two fathers shouted together.

They leaped into battle against Jade Master Shifu.

"We've got this, son!" Li assured him.

"Go, Dads!" Po cheered.

He jumped up on another rooftop and saw that the remaining jombies were all tied up in battle with the pandas—and losing. Po pumped his fist.

"We got 'em now!" he said.

Back at the ice wall, Kai struggled to keep track of the battle as he saw it through the eyes of all his jombies. He saw a crazy jumble of ribbons and nunchucks and dumplings and big, furry, squeezing arms. It was too much.

"Stop! Stop! Enough!" he cried.

Po knew the jombies were not going to be a problem anymore. There was only one thing left to do.

"Let's finish this," he said.

He dove down from the rooftop and landed past the waterfall into a pile of snow. He rolled and rolled down the hill, turning into a giant panda snowball. He hurtled over the ice toward Kai. Mr. Ping and Li looked on anxiously.

Boom! The snowball hit Kai and exploded. When the snowflakes cleared, Po was pressed against Kai, his pinky raised in the air, ready to strike with the Wuxi Finger Hold. Po had used the powerful move to annihilate the evil Tai Lung in his very first battle with a big bad guy. Nobody could escape the Wuxi Finger Hold. It was a massive, powerful display of kung fu awesomeness.

"Sorry, buddy," Po told Kai. "Gotta send you back to the Spirit Realm."

He dropped his pinky on Kai's finger. "Skadoosh."

Po waited for the spectacular explosion of golden light . . . but nothing happened.

"Okay, that didn't work. Let me try one more time," he said. "Skadoosh!"

Nothing.

"Skadoosh!"

Still nothing.

"Skadoosh, skadoosh, skadoosh!" Po cried, desperately repeating the move.

"Hold on, wait . . . it's working! No!" Kai wailed, but he was just psyching Po out. "No, it's not. Did Oogway teach you that little trick? Too bad. It only works on mortals. And I am a Spirit Warrior."

He called out to his jombies. "Come!"

The jade masters transformed into green streaks of light and flew back to Kai's belt. As each one returned, Kai gained energy. He began to pummel Po with mighty blows. Then he tossed Po into the air, jumped up, and delivered a powerful kick, sending Po flying.

Slam! Po hit the ground. The pandas, Tigress,

and Mr. Ping all rushed to his side. He lay there, still, looking battered and beaten.

"Son!" Li cried.

"Po!" Tigress knelt beside him.

"I was wrong," Po said weakly. "I'm sorry. Run . . . Run!"

CHAPTER 18
Po's Sacrifice

Nobody ran. Everybody stood by Po.

Kai's chain blades struck the ground behind Po, pulling Kai with them. He yanked the chain blades back to his hands. Then he looked down at Oogway's amulet and laughed.

"So, Oogway, this was the one destined to stop me?" he taunted.

He loomed over Po.

"I will have his chi," he promised, and then nodded toward the other pandas. "And all of theirs."

He hurled out one of the chain blades. It cut a groove into the ground around Po and the other pandas. Smiling, he took another step closer to Po.

Po looked around at his friends and loved ones. He had failed them. He couldn't defeat Kai. He just wasn't powerful enough.

"And you, you really thought you could send *me* back to the Spirit Realm?" Kai asked boastfully. "You're just a stupid mortal."

A light went on inside Po's head. "It only works on mortals. . . ." Po realized he didn't have to fail. He could save them all.

Well, almost all.

Po turned back to Kai.

"You're right, I can't send you there," he said. "But I can take you there."

Then he borrowed a trick from Master Shifu. He pointed behind Kai. "What's that?"

Kai turned in the direction Po was pointing, but there was nothing there. In an instant, Po leaped up and landed on Kai with his arms wrapped around him.

"Po?" Tigress asked, her eyes wide.

Po raised a pinky and looked and his family.

He smiled, then . . .

"Skadoosh."

Po dropped the pinky on his own finger.

"Son!" Li and Mr. Ping yelled.

"No!" wailed Kai.

BOOM! The power of the Wuxi Finger Hold rocked the mountain with a huge explosion of golden light, blinding the villagers, Tigress, and Mr. Ping. As the light faded, peach-blossom petals rained to the ground.

Po and Kai were gone. In the spot where they had stood was a yin-and-yang symbol made of peach petals.

"What happened? Where's Po?" Li said, his eyes filled with shock.

"He took Kai away," Tigress said softly. "He saved us."

"He saved us," said Mr. Ping. "But who's saving him?"

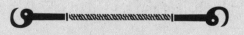

When Po opened his eyes, he found himself in a land filled with clouds and mountain debris.

"Whoa, the Spirit Realm!" he said. "It worked!"

Po looked down and realized he was sitting on top of Kai.

"Get off me, you . . ." Kai's voice trailed off as he grumbled, trying to squeeze out from under Po. He looked surprised when he saw the clouds. "You brought me back?"

"Don't blame me," Po said. "I tried to finish this in the regular realm."

Kai's eyes narrowed. "Then we'll finish it here!"

His chain blades shot out, and Po dodged them.

"Whoa!" Po cried.

But Kai's blades had latched on to a floating temple. He yanked the chains and sent the building hurtling toward Po.

Bam! It hit Po from behind and pushed him toward Kai, whose massive fist was waiting for him. *Pow!* He delivered a strong punch to Po's nose.

Kai quickly wrapped his chains around Po. He held out his hands and started to take Po's chi from him. Helpless, Po watched as his feet began to turn to jade. The jade crept up to his knees and then his belly, until it reached his face.

Back in the mortal realm, Li picked up handfuls of peach blossoms.

"Come on, son, fight," he said. He turned to the others. "We have to help him. Everyone, gather around! That's it, come in close. We can do this!"

Li felt an energy pulsing from the peach blossoms. Po's energy. Li knew it deep down. In the depths of his spirit, something ancient kicked in.

He brought his hands together, like he had seen the pandas do in the scroll. The other pandas gathered around him and mimicked his moves.

"Po," Li said. "You taught us who we were meant to be."

Li pushed his right hand forward, and his palm began to glow.

"A father," he said.

A glowing panda paw print appeared on Po's chest.

Tigress pushed her hand forward. "A friend."

Bao pushed his hand forward. "A dumpling kicker."

Big Fun performed the move. "A hugger."

Grandma Panda added her hand. "A lethal fighting machine."

Every panda in the village gathered chi and pushed it toward the flower petals. As they did, more and more glowing prints appeared on Po's jade body.

"A kung fu chick," said Mei Mei.

"A Stripy Baby," said Lei Lei.

Mr. Ping joined in. "A father."

Every hand in the village was now pointing at the peach-blossom petals. Every hand was glowing with beautiful chi.

The glowing handprints became brighter and brighter on Po's chest. The flower petals began to swirl . . . and the jade entombing Po exploded into pieces!

The force sent a shocked Kai flying backward.

"Noooooooooo!" he wailed.

CHAPTER 19
Po the Spirit Warrior

Po opened his eyes. He was still in the Spirit Realm. But he was no jombie! He could feel a straw hat on top of his head, and he wore a long cloak. It was the outfit he always wore when he imagined himself as a legendary hero.

"Whoa, that's cool."

He jumped up and began to move his hands in graceful swishing motions. He wasn't sure how he knew what to do—but he knew. Golden chi trailed his hand movements like ripples in the water, forming beautiful shapes. Kai stared in awe.

"Who *are* you?" he asked.

"I've been asking the same question. Am I the son of a panda? The son of a goose? A student? A teacher? Turns out I'm *all* of them. I *am* the Dragon Warrior!" Po said.

Then the golden chi shapes came together to become a huge, glowing dragon of chi! Po was part of the dragon, at its very heart, as the golden light swirled around him. "Get it? See the giant dragon? Hah! This is awesome!"

He waved his right arm, and the giant chi dragon waved his arm. He could control it!

Po flew through the air with the dragon's wings. Sweet!

"Get ready to feel the thunder!" he yelled, and he chomped his teeth. The dragon opened its huge mouth and chomped its teeth, too.

"Wahoo!" Po cheered.

Kai hurled a chain blade at Po. *Snap!* The dragon caught the chain in its glowing teeth and yanked Kai toward him.

"Butt Slap!" Po yelled, naming his new move.

He wiggled his butt and the dragon's tail lashed out, sending Kai crashing into the floating mountains.

"Perhaps a bit of lunch, 'cause I'm starving." Po slurped like he was eating noodles, and the dragon slurped in the chain blade. It evaporated inside the dragon's glowing belly. Po happily rubbed his tummy.

With a growl, Kai launched at Po again. Po flew the chi dragon right toward him, and the tail struck out at Kai, sending him tumbling away. He lashed out with his remaining chain blade, but couldn't make contact.

"Heads up!" Po shouted. The dragon swooped down at Kai and snatched the second blade in its mouth. He flew past a floating chunk of rock, sending Kai smashing into it, and then another and another. Finally the dragon swallowed the blade, and it dissolved inside the golden light, just like the other one had.

Kai glared at Po. "It took me five hundred years

to take Oogway's chi," he said. "I'll have yours if it takes me five hundred more!"

"Chitty chitty chat chat. Chitchat!" Po said. Behind him, the dragon mimed along with him.

Kai leaped at him again, but Po just smiled serenely.

"What's given is more powerful than what can be taken. This chi was given to me. So now I give it to you. All of it."

Po performed the same chi move that all his friends had done in the village when they saved him from Kai. When he pushed his hand forward, the dragon dived, shooting through Po and into Kai, overloading him with the power he wanted so very much.

One by one, the jade amulets detached from his belt and floated up and away. The Oogway amulet detached, and Kai desperately grasped for it.

"No!" he cried.

As the last of the dragon's tail vanished into Kai's body, there was an explosion of chi, and Kai was gone.

CHAPTER 20
Where's Po?

Back in the Panda Village, sunlight streamed down from the sky above. Tigress, Mr. Ping, and all of the pandas looked at the swirling peach petals in awe. In the center, they could see the jade amulets returning from the Spirit Realm.

The first amulet appeared and transformed back into Master Shifu—normal and completely un-jaded!

Four amulets appeared right on top of him and transformed back into Mantis, Monkey, Crane, and Viper!

"We're back!" Viper cheered, as they all tried to untangle themselves from the pile.

Monkey grabbed Mantis. "Bestie!"

"Monkey!" Mantis cried. He looked dazed. "I'm still green! It didn't work! Oh, wait . . . that's my normal green."

More jade amulets appeared, until all of the fallen masters had returned.

All but one.

Li rushed to the Furious Five. "What about Po?" he asked.

"He's not here?" asked Viper.

They all looked around anxiously.

"Po? Po?" Mr. Ping called. He sighed. "Why isn't he back?"

Po was still in the Spirit Realm. His mighty dragon of awesomeness had faded, and now he peacefully hovered in the air. The Oogway amulet floated toward him. In a flash of light, the amulet transformed into the spirit of Oogway.

He was wreathed in a golden glow.

"Dragon Warrior," Oogway said.

"Oogway?" Po asked, flipping around to face him. "Whoa, no way! I can't believe it! You're extra shiny!"

"As are you," Oogway replied.

"I know, right?" Po said, touching his cloak. "It's, like, the best cape ever! When I run with it, then it looks really cool."

"It suits you," Oogway said. "You've grown."

Po patted his tummy. "Yeah, I gotta lay off the panda buffet."

"Grown *up*," Oogway corrected him. "You finally became the panda you were always meant to be. As I hoped you would when I sent the message to your father." Oogway waved his hand, and the two of them landed gently in a boat on a golden lake below.

Po's eyes lit up. "*You* sent the universe mail! Whoa!"

Oogway nodded. "Yes. Because the universe needed you."

The boat stopped at a floating island with a peach tree on it. Po and Oogway got out of the boat.

"The universe needed *me*?" Po asked.

Oogway chuckled. "You helped save the world from Kai. That's a pretty good start."

"But how did you know I could?" Po asked.

"On the first day we met, I saw the future of kung fu . . . and the past," Oogway replied. "I saw the panda who could unite them both. That is why I chose you, Po. Both sides of the yin and yang. And my true successor."

He handed Po the gnarled staff that he carried.

"Me? I can't take that," said Po.

"Just take it," said Oogway. "I have a bigger one."

Slowly, Po took the staff. He stared at it for a second, and then started to twirl it like a battle staff before he settled down.

"Now what do we do?" he asked.

"You tell me," Oogway replied.

Peach blossoms began to swirl around Oogway.

"No, Oogway, don't go!" Po cried.

But Oogway reappeared on a nearby tree branch.

"I'm not going anywhere," Oogway said. "I live here."

Po was relieved. "Oh, right."

"It's *you* who must decide whether to stay or go," Oogway told him.

"Wait . . . I can go back?" Po asked.

"Who knows?" said Oogway. "I've never tried."

Po looked down at the staff he was holding. He used it to draw a yin-and-yang symbol in the golden water of the lake.

"Wow," said Po.

Then there was a flash of light.

CHAPTER 21
One Big Happy Family

In the mortal realm, everyone waited, hoping for some sign of Po.

They weren't disappointed.

First came the peach blossoms. They gracefully swirled down to the ground, and where the swarm of petals had all fallen, Po appeared in midair, still wearing his cape and heroic garb. The pandas gasped in awe . . .

. . . until Po's cool clothes disappeared and he landed on the ground with a *splat!*

Mr. Ping and Li rushed to him.

"Dads!" Po cried.

"Don't you go disappearing in petals ever again!" Mr. Ping scolded.

"We . . . we thought we lost you," Li said.

"No. You saved me," Po told him.

The two fathers hugged and kissed and squeezed him. Tears of joy streamed down their faces.

Po turned to the pandas.

"You all did," he said. "Come here!"

All the pandas came running up, wrapping Po in a huge group hug.

"Hugs!" shouted Big Fun as he dove in.

Po rolled his eyes as Big Fun and the others released him.

Shifu approached next, proud of his old student. Po bowed.

"The student has truly become the teach— Wait, where did you get that?" Shifu asked, noticing the staff in Po's hand.

"Oh, this?" Po replied with a shrug. "Oogway gave it to me in the Spirit Realm."

Master Shifu sighed. "Of course he did."

Po whispered, "I think I mastered chi."

Master Shifu sighed even harder. "Of course you did." And he didn't even have to sit in a cave for thirty years!

But then the look on Master Shifu's face changed. "Can you . . . teach me?"

Po smiled.

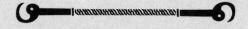

Afterward, the pandas in the Panda Village came to the Valley of Peace. The pandas were happy to be reunited with their long-lost Po, and Mr. Ping was happy to be reunited with the new batch of panda customers he'd found for the noodle shop.

The Jade Palace was opened for kung fu lessons to everyone. Not only did the pandas and villagers attend, but masters from far and wide came to learn the secrets of chi that Po passed on to his students.

As for Po, he had never felt so happy: He had friends, family, and two dads who loved him.

Sweet!